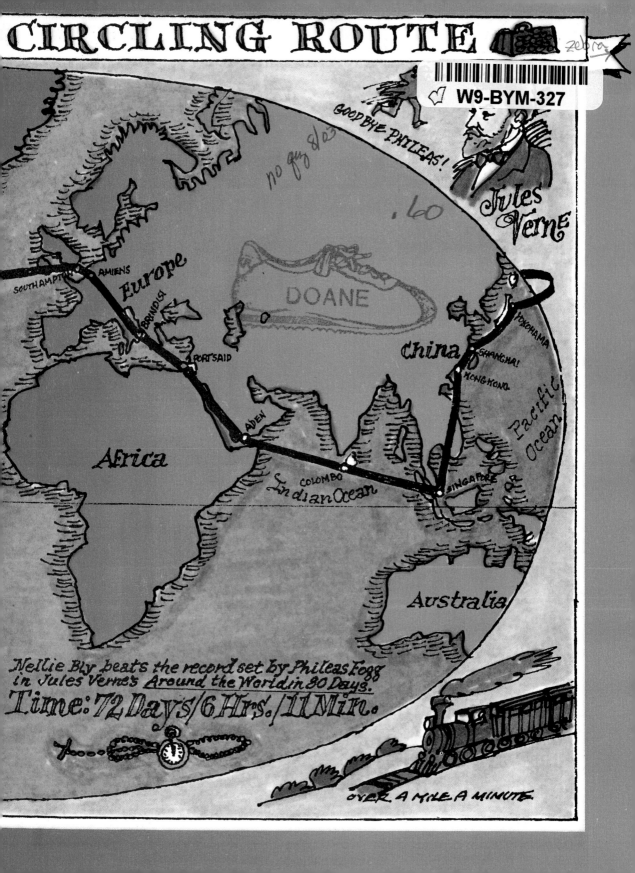

ELIZABETH ENJOYS READING & WRITING.

Robert Quackenbush
Stop the Presses, Nellie's Got a Scoop!
A Story of Nellie Bly

SIMON & SCHUSTER BOOKS FOR YOUNG READERS

Published by Simon & Schuster
New York · London · Toronto · Sydney · Tokyo · Singapore.

SIMON & SCHUSTER BOOKS FOR YOUNG READERS

Simon & Schuster Building, Rockefeller Center

1230 Avenue of the Americas, New York, New York 10020

Copyright © 1992 by Robert Quackenbush. All rights reserved including the right

of reproduction in whole or in part in any form. SIMON & SCHUSTER BOOKS FOR

YOUNG READERS is a trademark of Simon & Schuster.

Designed by Robert Quackenbush.

The text of this book is set in Times Roman.

The illustrations were done in pen and ink on watercolor paper with color and

black half tone overlays on waxed rice paper.

Manufactured in the United States of America

10 9 8 7 6 5 4 3 2 1   (pbk) 10 9 8 7 6 5 4 3 2 1

Library of Congress Cataloging-in-Publication Data

Quackenbush, Robert M.   Stop the presses, Nellie's got a scoop! : a story of Nellie Bly /

by Robert Quackenbush.   Summary: Recounts the events in the life of the

crusading reporter.   1. Bly, Nellie, 1864 – 1922 — Juvenile literature.   2. Women journalists —

United States — Biography — Juvenile literature.   2. Journalism — United States — History —

Juvenile literature.   [1. Bly, Nellie, 1864 – 1922.   2. Journalists.]   PN4874.B59033   1992

070′.92 — dc20   [B]   91-44087   CIP

ISBN: 0-671-76090-4   ISBN: 0-671-76091-2 (pbk)

There was once a girl named Elizabeth Cochran, later known as Nellie Bly. She was born on May 5, 1864, in Cochran's Mills, Pennsylvania, a small town named after her father, Michael Cochran, a wealthy businessman, lawyer, and judge. When Elizabeth was six, her father died and left her mother, Mary Jane Kennedy Cochran, a wealthy widow. Elizabeth grew up in a big house with five older brothers, one younger brother, and a younger sister. Elizabeth was much more spirited and independent than her sister. She competed with her brothers. She rode horseback, climbed trees, and played sports like they did. But what she most enjoyed was reading and writing. She dreamed of being a real-life author one day. She even added an *e* to her last name because she thought Cochrane would look better on a book cover.

By the time Elizabeth was 20, her family's wealth had dwindled. The large Cochran home was sold and the family scattered. Elizabeth, with her mother and sister, moved to Pittsburgh and lived in a series of boarding houses. Elizabeth had to find work. She still longed for a career as a writer. She wrote several articles, but was unable to sell them. In those days, writing was considered a man's profession. About the only meaningful careers that were available to women were nursing and teaching. But those jobs were scarce. Women were not even allowed to vote. Elizabeth looked everywhere for something interesting to do. Her only job offer was to wash and iron clothes in a hot, steaming laundry. She was very discouraged.

ELIZABETH, AGE 20, LOOKS FOR WORK IN PITTSBURGH.

One day Elizabeth happened to read an article in the Pittsburgh *Dispatch* written by Erasmus Wilson. Wilson poked fun at young women like herself who sought careers in what were then considered male professions. Elizabeth sat down and wrote a furious letter to the editor of the *Dispatch*, George Madden. She told him from firsthand experience what it was like to be a woman living in 1885 and how impossible it was to find meaningful work. She signed the letter "Lonely Orphan Girl" because that is what she felt like. Madden published the letter. At the same time, he placed an ad inviting the writer to identify herself. Elizabeth saw the notice. She went to the *Dispatch* and introduced herself to Madden and Wilson. To her surprise, Madden offered her a job as a reporter. Elizabeth gladly accepted. Her bold letter made her dream come true.

ELIZABETH VISITS *THE DISPATCH.*

NEWSBOYS ANNOUNCE "NELLIE BLY'S" SHOCKING STORY.

Elizabeth's first article as a reporter for the *Dispatch* pleaded for better marriage laws. Elizabeth wrote that marriage should be a free choice for women and that they should not be pressured into it by members of their family or society. She believed that a woman should have the right to divorce her husband if he mistreated her. Divorce was considered a scandal at that time. It was a subject that was discussed in hushed tones and never in mixed company. For this reason, Madden suggested to her that she use a pen name to protect herself and her family from negative public reaction. Elizabeth chose the name "Nellie Bly," the title of a popular song by Stephen Foster. The outspoken article appeared on the front page of the *Dispatch* under the headline "Mad Marriages." The moment it was published, it became the talk of Pittsburgh. Some readers believed that the daring new reporter was a man. The pen name stuck. From then on Elizabeth was known as Nellie Bly, crusading reporter.

15

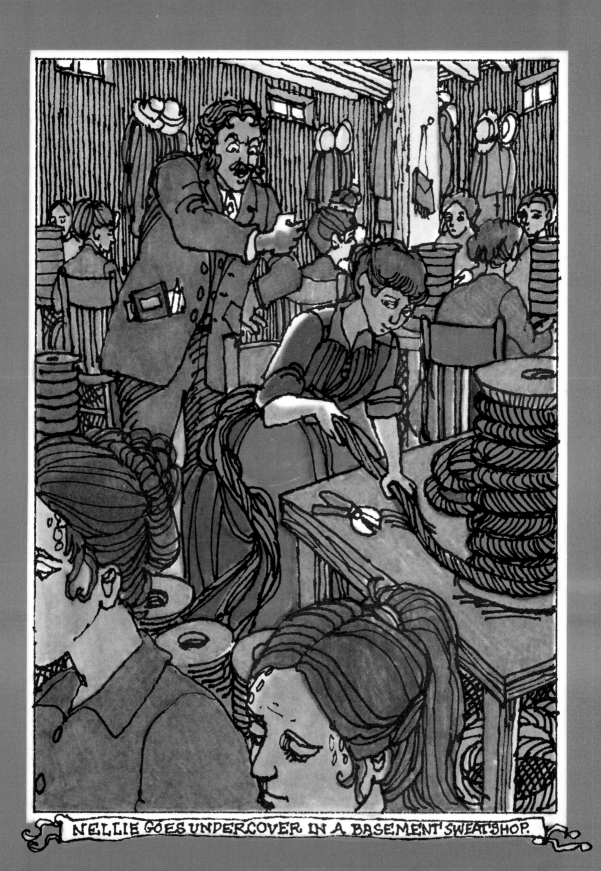

NELLIE GOES UNDERCOVER IN A BASEMENT SWEATSHOP.

Nellie's next articles were featured in the Sunday editions of the *Dispatch*. They were an illustrated series entitled "Our Workshop Girls." To gather her material, Nellie became an undercover investigator. She would visit establishments disguised as one of the workers, doing backbreaking labor alongside the other employees. She wrote about dangerous working conditions and rat-infested factories. She wrote about women who toiled from early morning until late at night for barely enough money to survive. She wrote about children who were being made to work like slaves. Nothing kept her from doing a story. Soon she became Pittsburgh's best-known journalist. Her articles brought about improved working conditions for women and stricter labor laws for children. At 21 years of age, she was one of the most important people in the city.

17

But then, abruptly, Nellie Bly's articles about working women ended. The reason was not clear. Perhaps Madden of the *Dispatch* was worried about losing advertisers because of the daring series. Whatever the reason, Nellie soon found herself limited to writing about fashion, society, and flower shows. She was impatient with these duties. She wished for something more exciting, like traveling to exotic lands as a correspondent. The opportunity came in 1886 when she was assigned to write about a team of officials from Mexico who were visiting Pittsburgh. Her articles about the visit so impressed the officials that they invited her to come to their country. Although Nellie did not know Spanish, she was eager to go. She was able to convince Madden that eyewitness accounts about Mexican life would boost newspaper sales. He agreed to the idea because little was then known about Mexico in the United States. With that, Nellie boarded a train with her mother and headed west.

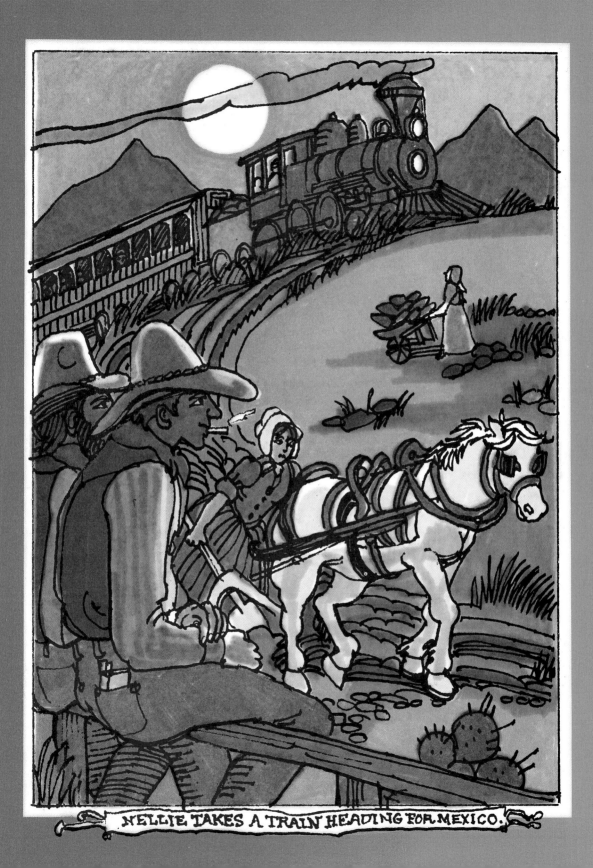

NELLIE TAKES A TRAIN HEADING FOR MEXICO.

What Nellie saw during her travels moved her to write passionately. About the American West she wrote: "For the first time I saw women plowing while their lords and masters sat on a fence smoking. I have never longed for anything so much as I did to shove those lazy fellows off." About Mexico she wrote; "The husband puts his wife in his home which is henceforth the extent of her life." She had outspoken comments about other injustices, too. Toward the end of her journey she wrote a seething article about the lack of freedom of speech in Mexico at the time, and how reporters could be thrown in jail for saying things against the government. Soon afterwards she received an anonymous threatening note. She decided that it was time to go home. Nellie was worried that she would not be able to cross the border with her writings about Mexico. Luckily, the suitcase that contained them was not inspected by guards. Her book, *Six Months in Mexico*, was published in 1888 under her own name, Elizabeth Cochrane.

NELLIE AND HER MOTHER ESCAPE FROM MEXICO.

NELLIE WAITS IN THE OFFICES OF *THE WORLD.*

Upon her return to Pittsburgh, Nellie longed for further adventure. She quit her job at the *Dispatch* and moved to New York. She wanted to work for the most exciting newspaper of the time, which was Joseph Pulitzer's *The World*. Pulitzer sought to publish scoops which would promote positive social change. But Nellie could not find work there or at any other newspaper in New York. No one had any use for a woman journalist, not even one with proven abilities. Months went by. Finally Nellie marched down to the offices of *The World* and refused to leave until Pulitzer saw her. Hours later, Pulitzer met with her and agreed to hire her if she could pass a test assignment. Nellie offered to go as an undercover reporter to the notorious insane asylum on Blackwell's Island in New York's East River. (Today, Blackwell's Island is a residential area called Roosevelt Island.) Her idea was to pose as an inmate of the asylum for one week in order to report on the bad conditions there. Pulitzer agreed to let her try the dangerous assignment.

NELLIE UNDERCOVER AT BLACKWELL'S ISLAND ASYLUM.

Nellie managed to get herself sent to Blackwell's Island by pretending that she had lost her memory. She was locked in a crowded room. Sleep was impossible because of all the noise. The dreadful food consisted of stringy bits of meat and moldy bread. A bath meant being doused with a bucket of cold water. At first Nellie feared the patients, but she soon learned she had more to fear from abusive staff members. She saw evidence of inmates who had been beaten. She also saw inmates she believed did not belong there, such as a woman who couldn't speak English well enough to be understood. Nellie was worried that she might be trapped there herself. Luckily for her, a lawyer at *The World* got her released after ten days. Her front-page story shocked New York and gained national attention. As a result, the treatment of patients on Blackwell's Island improved dramatically. In addition, dozens of other mental hospitals across the country were investigated and reformed. Nellie had done it again with another scoop!

NELLIE FLEES WITH EVIDENCE FOR ANOTHER SCOOP.

Nellie's scoop made her an overnight celebrity in New York. Pulitzer hired her, of course, and her next story was a sensational exposé of the city's terrible prison conditions. To write it, Nellie had herself committed to a prison by having a friend accuse her of robbery. Her powerful story led to separate prisons for male and female prisoners and to the hiring of female attendants for female prisoners. For another story, Nellie posed as an invalid to investigate sloppy medical treatment for the poor. She even took on political organizations. She wanted to expose corrupt lobbyist Edward Phelps who had power to kill or save any bill that went before the New York State legislature. When a bill came up that would restrain manufacturers from producing potentially dangerous medicines, Nellie went to see Phelps at his Albany hotel. She posed as the wife of a medicine manufacturer who would lose his business if the bill were passed. She talked Phelps into accepting a bribe to stop the bill. Then she got him to give her a receipt before she wrote him a check. After he handed her the receipt, she pretended to go get her checkbook in another room, but fled instead. Her scoop ruined Phelps and saved the bill.

After two years of writing exciting news stories, Nellie looked for a new challenge. She decided to go around the world. Her plan was to try to beat the record of French novelist Jules Verne's fictional character Phileas Fogg in *Around the World in Eighty Days*. She proposed the idea to Pulitzer and he agreed that such a trip would gain a lot of readers. Nellie took off with a single suitcase in hand. The whole world followed the progress of her journey by ship and train with excitement. People cheered her along the way. In France she had tea with Jules Verne who wished her well. In Hong Kong a cannon was fired in her honor. Crossing the Pacific on the *Oceanic*, a sign was placed over the engine that said, "For Nellie Bly, we'll win or die!" And win she did! On January 25, 1890, she returned to New York exactly 72 days, 6 hours, and 11 minutes after she left. She traveled 21,740 miles and broke Phileas Fogg's record. Congratulatory telegrams were showered on her from all over the world, including one from Jules Verne, who had thought she could not do it. Nellie Bly was an international hero.

NELLIE WITH HER SUITCASE IN HAND IN HONG KONG.

Nellie's celebrated globe-trotting feat led to wealth and more fame. She stopped working at *The World*, went on speaking tours, endorsed products for advertisements, and wrote a book entitled *Nellie Bly's Book: Around the World in 72 Days*. However, wealth and fame were no match for her thirst for exciting journalism. Three years later, in 1893, she returned to *The World*. She kept on writing scoops about New York, but she also wrote about what was happening in other parts of the country. She went to Chicago in 1894 to report on a Pullman railroad strike. When she saw the poor and cramped company homes for the workers she wrote: "I became the bitterest striker of them all." The next year she traveled to Nebraska to write about the plight of ranchers who were suffering from a series of droughts. On a return train, Nellie met Robert L. Seaman, founder of the Iron Clad Manufacturing Company, one of America's largest hardware producers. Although Seaman was a number of years older than Nellie, who was now 30, they had an immediate liking for one another. Soon afterwards, in April 1895, *The World* announced their marriage.

30

NELLIE MEETS INDUSTRIALIST ROBERT L. SEAMAN.

After the wedding, Nellie abandoned her newspaper career to assume the role of Mrs. Elizabeth Cochrane Seaman, society hostess. She staged elaborate parties at the couple's Manhattan home and at their estate in Catskill, New York. But this was not totally satisfying to Nellie Bly. She was more interested in helping her husband with his business. She advised him on how to build good employer/worker relationships based on what she had learned as an undercover reporter. Nine years after they were married, Robert Seaman died of a heart attack. But Nellie was experienced enough by then to run the business by herself. She increased Iron Clad's hardware output and formed other divisions, including a multimillion dollar steel drum plant. Her workers numbered 1,500. She paid the women the same as the men and provided her workers with health care and other benefits for their families.

32

NELLIE MANAGES IRON CLAD MANUFACTURING.

NELLIE RETURNS TO HER FIRST LOVE.

Nellie's success in industry lasted only a few years. By 1912, she was near financial ruin. She discovered that some of her employees had been stealing money from the company for a long time. Then came lawsuits and creditors clamoring to be paid. One year later, Iron Clad was forced into bankruptcy. Heartsick, she went to Austria in 1914 to rest for a few weeks. But while she was there, most of Europe suddenly erupted in World War I. She was trapped in Vienna until the war ended, in 1918. When she finally got back home, she had to start all over again at 55 years of age. The ever courageous Nellie Bly returned to her first love—the newspaper world. She was hired by the New York *Journal* and given her own features column. Her last great scoop, in January 1920, was an impassioned plea for an end to death in the electric chair. She wrote it after witnessing a public execution at New York's Sing Sing prison. She didn't manage to get the law changed, but she drew attention to the fact that it should be changed. Decades later it was. Today there is no death penalty in New York State, as well as in most of the United States.

Nellie Bly died suddenly, on January 27, 1922, from pneumonia. She was 58 years old. Thus ended a career of magnificent reporting that stirred the public's conscience. For her stories, Nellie went to slums and factories and wrote angrily about tenement landlords and sweatshop owners who let people live and work in cold, dark, rat-infested rooms. She visited city hospitals and prisons as an undercover investigator and wrote about deplorable conditions at these institutions. With her mighty pen, she also fought against prejudices toward women and encouraged women to try new, adventurous things. Her powerful words pointed the way for many reforms and rescued countless people from misery and injustice. Besides being America's first newspaper woman, Nellie Bly is still regarded by many members of the press as the nation's best reporter.

36

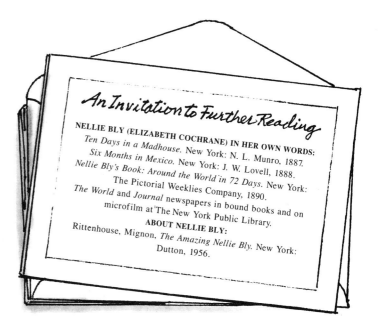

An Invitation to Further Reading

NELLIE BLY (ELIZABETH COCHRANE) IN HER OWN WORDS:

Ten Days in a Madhouse. New York: N. L. Munro, 1887.

Six Months in Mexico. New York: J. W. Lovell, 1888.

Nellie Bly's Book: Around the World in 72 Days. New York: The Pictorial Weeklies Company, 1890.

The World and *Journal* newspapers in bound books and on microfilm at The New York Public Library.

ABOUT NELLIE BLY:

Rittenhouse, Mignon, *The Amazing Nellie Bly.* New York: Dutton, 1956.

'ROUND THE WORLD

Nellie Bly

THE WORLD'S GLOBE CIRCLER

GAME RULES:

Speeding Across the Atlantic

ANY NUMBER CAN PLAY. VOYAGERS MAY USE COINS OR COLORED PIECES OF CARDBOARD. THROW DICE. A THROW OF ONE PUTS THE VOYAGER ON THE 1ST DAY, A THROW OF SIX PUTS THE PLAYER ON THE 6TH DAY, ETC. FOLLOW DIRECTIONS GIVEN ON THE